To all great things that were once small and
all small things that will someday be great – JDS

For Roan and Calder (and their wonderful parents) – JR

Phaidon Press Limited
Regent's Wharf
All Saints Street
London N1 9PA

Phaidon Press Inc.
65 Bleecker Street
New York, NY 10012

phaidon.com

First published 2018
© 2018 Phaidon Press Limited
Text copyright © Joshua David Stein
Illustrations copyright © Julia Rothman

Artwork illustrated using collage and ink
Typeset in Basilia Regular and Pedrera Italic Bold

ISBN 978 0 7148 7631 3
001-0418

A CIP catalogue record for this book is available from
the British Library and the Library of Congress.

Designed by Meagan Bennett

Printed in China

Picture credits: Malbork Castle: Rosmarie Wirz/Getty images, St. Basil's
Cathedral: Jose Vilchez/Alamy Stock Photo, The Ark: robertharding/Alamy
Stock Photo, Malwiya Minaret: De Agostini Picture Library/Getty images,
Park East Synagogue: Meagan Bennett, Great Wall of China: Zoonar GmbH/
Alamy Stock Photo, Levittown: Joseph Scherschel/Getty images, Mahabodhi
Temple: Hakbong Kwon/Alamy Stock Photo, Grosvenor Estate: Homer Sykes/
Alamy Stock Photo, Red Brick Cottage: Rocco Fasano/Getty images

BRICK

Who Found Herself in Architecture

words by Joshua David Stein

illustrated by Julia Rothman

When Brick was just a baby, tall buildings amazed her.
She wondered how anything could grow so big.

"Great things begin with small bricks," her mother said,
"Look around, you'll see."

So Brick looked around. She saw that the homes on her street were made out of bricks just like her. When she looked closer, she saw that the fire station, the schoolhouse, and the post office, which all seemed so grand to her, were made of brick too.

She wondered if this was the same on the next street and the street after that, and in the next town and the town after that. Were there bricks across the ocean, in lands faraway? Brick wondered where she fit in to all of this. What great thing might she become?

As Brick grew, so did her curiosity. Soon, but not too soon, she was old enough to embark upon a journey of her own, to find her place in the world.

So on a clear, moonlit night, Brick set sail.

It was a long and dangerous voyage, but
Brick proved to be brave.

By the time she made landfall, Brick was hardened by the sun
and heartened by her own strength. She began to explore at once.

First, she visited a castle on the banks of a river, with slits for shooting arrows, and high walls all around.

Malbork
Castle

Next, she visited
another very old castle,
this one built in the
middle of a desert.

The Ark

But as she peered at the walls of
these castles, she saw the scars
that years of fighting had caused.

Brick did not want to fight.
So she moved on.

She journeyed to
fantastic churches,

Saint Basil's
Cathedral

spiraling mosques,

Malwiya
Minaret

Park East
Synagogue

and splendid synagogues, until …

…she arrived at a towering
Buddhist temple nestled
among the fig trees.

These places of worship filled her with awe, for their beauty was divine, but they did not call out to her.

And so she kept going.

Mahabodhi Temple

She walked atop walls that snaked as far as she could see.

But walls divide, and that was not what Brick wanted to do. So her journey continued.

Great Wall of China

Brick loved the hustle and bustle of family life. Perhaps she could become a home and listen to the laughter of children as they played, keep them warm as they slept. So Brick visited apartment buildings on crowded city streets, where homes were stacked on top of one another.

Grosvenor
Estate

In smaller towns, she walked
by rows of neat brick houses
that looked exactly alike.

Levittown

Red Brick Cottage

In the country, she passed a single brick cottage with a chimney billowing smoke and a welcome glow in the windows.

But homes eventually empty and hearths grow cold. "No," Brick shivered, "I will not be a home, either." What was there left to be? Brick lost hope.

As she walked, she thought of her journey thus far and all that she had seen.

When she could go no farther, she sat down and thought some
more. "Great things begin with small bricks," she repeated.
Then, she let go of the words and just felt the feeling.

Day became night, but still
Brick didn't stir.

And then suddenly, it dawned on her.
Maybe Brick could just stay right where she was.
After all, her journey had led her exactly here.
Perhaps *here* was the perfect place to be.

And so she became part of a wide
and lovely path, along which other
bricks could travel to find their
own places in the world.

For not only do great things begin with small bricks, but great journeys do too.

About the architecture in this book

Malbork Castle | Malbork, Poland

Built more than 700 years ago by medieval knights, Malbork Castle is the world's largest brick castle, and the largest brick building in all of Europe. For many years, it was home to hundreds of soldier monks called the Teutonic Knights. Today, it is a museum that hosts concerts, tours, and art exhibitions.

Saint Basil's Cathedral | Moscow, Russia

One of the most famous churches in the world, Saint Basil's Cathedral sits in the middle of Moscow's Red Square. Built under Ivan the Terrible in 1555, the building is meant to look like a bonfire rising to the sky, though today, it's known for its bright colors and its nine domes that look like onions!

The Ark | Bukhara, Uzbekistan

Nearly 3,000 people once lived inside this ancient fortress, including a king, his royal court, and all those who served them. The walls withstood many attacks, including one by Gengh Khan in the 13th century and another by the Bolsheviks in the 20th century. It is now a museum

Malwiya Minaret | Samarra, Iraq

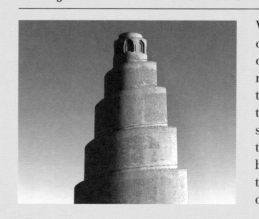

When it was built in the 9th century, the Great Mosque of Samarra was the largest mosque in the world. Now all that remains is this minaret, or tower, whose name means "snai shell" or "spiral." Minarets like these are used for calls to praye by Muslims. Sadly, in 2005, the top part of this one was badly damaged by a bomb.

rk East Synagogue | New York, NY, USA

The Park East Synagogue, a place for Jews to pray and learn, was built in 1890, but it looks even older. The style of the building is called Moorish Revival, which means the designs are based on the buildings of the Moors (Muslims) from the Middle Ages. Today, the synagogue is surrounded by modern apartment buildings, making it stand out even more!

eat Wall of China | China

The Great Wall of China is the longest wall in the world! It was built 2,300 years ago to protect China's northern borders from invasions. The Wall is actually a series of walls, some of which overlap. The earliest sections were made of stone and earth. However, a large part of it was built with brick during the Ming Empire in the 14th century.

vittown | Long Island, NY, USA

After World War II, many soldiers returned to the United States and needed homes for their families. In 1946, a developer named William Levitt turned an old potato field into America's first planned suburb. The identical houses were built in sections ahead of time, and were very quick to put together. It took only 16 minutes to construct one!

Mahabodhi Temple | Bodh Gaya, India

The Mahabodhi Temple is one of the oldest brick structures in India. It was build in the 6th century B.C.E. for Buddhist worship. Buddhists believe that the Buddha realized some pretty important things about the universe while sitting underneath the Bodhi (fig) tree that still grows at this temple today.

Grosvenor Estate | London, UK

When the famous architect Sir Edward Lutyens designed these affordable homes for workers in the 1920s, he tried to create the feeling of a village street in the heart of London. He used brick and white concrete to make a checkered pattern and built courtyards where children could play. Today, these apartments are still home to many families.

Red Brick Cottage | Woodbastwick, Norfolk, UK

This cottage, in a small town in the east of England, is made of red brick and timber (wood), with a roof made of thatched reeds. There are many cottages like this one all over the countryside of England. Some were built 700 years ago, back when families had only their hearths (fireplaces) to keep them warm.